Sherlock Holmes

and

The Texas Adventure

Written by Dicky Neely

Edited by Claire Ellul

Paperback ISBN 9781780923543
ePub ISBN 9781780923550
PDF ISBN 9781780923567

Published in the UK by MX Publishing
335 Princess Park Manor, Royal Drive,
London, N11 3GX
www.mxpublishing.co.uk

Cover design by www.staunch.com

I dedicate this book to my siblings, Jan and Blake, in Daingerfield, Texas, and Melinda, in Santa Barbara, California. Also to my son Brent, in Los Angeles, California and my daughter Trish and her family, in Longmont, Colorado. I love you all.

I also want to thank Claire Ellul for the wonderful job she did as my editor.

"You may all go to hell and I will go to Texas"

Davy Crockett in his farewell address to the U.S. Congress after losing his race for re-election to a third term.

Chapter 1 *A message from Texas*

It was cold, wet and blustery that October day as I returned to our rooms at Baker Street after a day spent at my practice. I quickly went up the stairs and found Holmes seated by the window gazing out at the street below. He was sitting by a table, covered with the detritus of recent experiments, wreathed in his customary cloud of smoke, as he curled up in his chair. He held a telegram in his hand, which he tapped up and down on the table top.

"I say, Holmes! The weather is utterly abominable today!"

"Is it? I hadn't noticed," replied Holmes with an air of detachment as I divested myself of my coat and hat. That gave me pause. We had had no recent cases to work on and I feared Holmes might revert to some of his former bad habits when the dreaded curse of boredom began to set in. But Holmes appeared keen, his eyes bright as he gazed out the window.

"You must have a new case. Nothing else would so enliven you on a day like this," I ventured.

"Possibly," he said. "Quite possibly." He handed me the telegram.

"Who is it from?" I asked.

"Read it out loud, if you please," Holmes replied.

"Mr. Holmes," I read, "You were referred to me by Mister Castle of New York, who you helped when he was in England.-STOP-Beg you come to Texas on important matter-STOP- More in post arriving 15th."

"Well, Watson. Today is the 15th and the post has arrived! I have yet to open it. Would you be so kind?"

Holmes reached out his arm with the palm turned up and with a slight wave bid me to open the missive and read the contents out loud.

The message read as follows:

> *My Dear Mr. Holmes,*
> *It is my utmost hope that you might consent to travel here to Texas, in the United States. I am faced with an urgent situation in regard to the disappearance of a close relative which has remained unsolved by the local authorities.*
> *I will pay whatever fee you ask and pay all expenses. I will provide lodgings here at my ranch if that suits you. In anticipation of your acceptance I have taken the liberty of leasing a small but fast packet steamer which awaits you at Portsmouth. If you accept please contact my agent in London, a Mr. Jared Thompson, his card is enclosed.*
> *Henrietta M. Royal,*
> *Rancho Royal, Texas*

"Would you like to go to Texas, Watson?" asked Holmes with a sly grin.

"Texas!" This was something different! "I have never contemplated going to Texas," I replied.

Holmes quickly reached for his well-worn copy of the *World Gazette* and turned to the "R's". He found the entry he sought and handed the volume to me.

"Here, Watson, read this."

"Hmmm…let's see. "Rancho Royal, Texas USA. A large ranch located in South Texas to the West of Corpus Christi and North of Brownsville. The ranch was founded in 1856 by Richard M. Royal and established as a large cattle ranching operation which has grown considerably since its inception to become one of the largest ranches in its area. Henrietta Royal, granddaughter of Richard M., is the current principal of the family and she runs the ranch and various business operations. These include a leather shop, a foundry, blacksmithing, animal husbandry and of course crops and cattle.""

I set the book down and glanced at Holmes, "Sounds like a very colorful and possibly well off client," I stated. "Texas; full of outlaws, Mexicans and cowboys! And very hot, I might add."

"So I take it you are not interested, Watson?"

"I didn't say that. It sounds fascinating. And besides, it would be a darn site warmer than it is here!"

3

Chapter 2 *Portsmouth*

The next morning we found ourselves in Portsmouth and found the office of Mr. Jared Taylor. He said he was expecting us and had taken the liberty of obtaining all of the necessary documents and the tickets for the trans-Atlantic passage.

"I have not yet agreed to take on this case as of yet. I still need more information. Such as how much time are we looking at? What about accommodations and necessary travel and a myriad other things?" Holmes said.

Mr. Taylor, who was an American, bade us sit down on his very comfortable, plush couch.

"Of course, Mr. Holmes. Ask anything you like."

"What is the nature of the problems Mrs. Royal desires my help to solve?

"That I don't know sir. I have here a packet with correspondence for you from Mrs. Royal. Of course this is confidential in nature and I have not opened it."

"Quite. Quite," said Holmes. "May I have the packet?"

"Certainly sir." And with that Taylor rose and turned to a wall safe behind his desk. He quickly opened it and from it withdrew a large Manila envelope addressed to Sherlock Holmes. The words extremely confidential were written largely on the front and back of the envelope.

"Here you are sir."

Holmes took the envelope and opened it. He withdrew some typewritten pages and looked them over quickly.

"Mr. Taylor," said Holmes. "Do you have a room where my colleague Dr. Watson, and I might discuss these papers in private?"

"Why yes sir, step this way." Taylor directed us to a small room with a desk and two chairs.

"Watson, would you be so kind as to read aloud the cover letter?"

Holmes handed me the letter. It was on stationery of a high quality paper and had the Double R brand (RR) emblazoned on it along with the words "Rancho Royal."

RR

I began reading.

"Dear Mr. Holmes:

My name is Henrietta Royal. I am the principal owner of the Rancho Royal and I desire your help in solving some strange and mysterious circumstances that have occurred here recently. The local authorities are stumped and have no ideas. I have heard of your work and your reputation from mutual acquaintances and I receive The Strand here, though a bit dated, and I have followed your adventures there as laid out by your friend Dr. Watson.

Here is a short version of the facts of the case. Early this past spring my grandson went missing. A long and careful search yielded nothing and the search was called off. No one knows what happened.

"Sounds a nasty business Holmes," I said as I glanced up at Holmes.

"Yes, yes, do go on," prompted Holmes.

I continued, "I have gone to great lengths to obtain your assistance and I hope you will accept my plea. If possible bring Doctor Watson as well. I am prepared to pay any fee you ask and

Mr. Taylor has a thousand pounds for your expenses, Of course ship passage is already taken care of. Pleas telegraph me as soon as possible as to your decision.

Sincerely,

Henrietta Royal."

"Well Watson, what do you make of it?"

"I think it sounds like troubled waters in Texas!"

"Are you up for it? Things are slow for us right now. Such a trip as this, along with a difficult case, might be just what the doctor ordered! No pun intended my dear friend," said Holmes.

Chapter 3 SS *Stephen F. Austin*

At that moment a change swept over Holmes' aquiline features, His expression became sharp and his eyes shone with anticipation. "Let's do it Watson!"

Turning to Mr. Taylor he said "Mr. Taylor we are on it. Please give us all of your help and cooperation for which we will be most grateful."

"Certainly. One moment."

Taylor returned to the safe and withdrew a second packet. It contained money, maps, books and more papers.

"I trust you both have passports already. Here are your visas, some pictures of Mrs. Royal, the ranch and other items which may prove useful. You will sail day after tomorrow at dawn on the *S.S. Stephen F. Austin*. The ship is docked presently at our dock, just down the quay from here. Want to take a look at it?"

"Why yes," exclaimed Holmes. "Let's have a look.

We left the office and walked a short distance to the docks where we saw the *SS Stephen F. Austin* moored there floating placidly at its berth.

The *Stephen F. Austin* was a trim steamer at about 300 feet in length and with one stack. The hull above the water line was white with black trim. The superstructure carried this scheme throughout.

"There she is sirs. A mighty nice looking ship I would say. She can do around 24 knots and rides the swell very well."

"And this was leased for us?" asked a bemused Holmes. "Money must be of little object!"

As we stood there a group of three ship's officers came down the gangway. Taylor motioned them to come over.

"Ah Mr. Holmes, this is Captain Johansen."

Holmes nodded to the seaman. "How do you do?"

Captain Johansen clicked his heels and nodded also. "Very well sir. Allow me to introduce my ship's officer's first mate Allen and second mate Jones."

"Gentlemen," said Holmes.

"You two must be very important to have our ship leased for your passage! Just let us know how we might make the voyage more pleasant. Good day sirs, pleasure to make your acquaintances," said the captain as they continued down the quay.

"He's a good and experienced captain Mr. Holmes," said Taylor. "He has a long record of successful employment and many voyages."

"I am glad to hear it," replied Holmes.

"Now gentlemen we have reserved rooms for you for the next two nights," said Taylor.

He led us on a short walk to the Jack Tar Inn where we soon found ourselves comfortably ensconced in adequate, if not comfortable rooms.

The next day and evening we spent some of our time exploring the Port of Portsmouth and the local environs.

We took our dinner in the Hotel dining room. We enjoyed fish and chips with vinegar and quaffed down a couple of beers. It was quite good fare.

"So where do you see this going Holmes? Surely the Royals must have accumulated a number of enemies while building such a ranch and their formidable holdings?" I asked.

"No doubt that is true Watson. I think we will gain some useful information and insight in the materials Mr. Taylor provided us."

Taylor's packet had included a few books, pamphlets, brochures and maps concerning Texas history, the history of Rancho Royal, the biography of Richard Royal and other assorted items, photographs etc. We passed those latter parts of the next evenings perusing this small library of Texana. We discovered that Richard M. Royal was a sea captain who had been engaged in the shipping of cattle hides from along the Gulf Coast of Texas and Mexico. His business had brought him to the then modest coastal village of Corpus Christi where a number of Packery houses and tanneries were located. There he became friends with several of the local cattle ranchers and tannery operators. Royal had made a number of hunting trips into the interior west and south of Corpus Christi and was well impressed with the availability and variety of wild game there. He also saw a huge potential for cattle grazing for which he saw a bright future.

Chapter 4 *A study in ranch building*

It was fascinating reading and the many illustrations and photographs were also of great interest. We read how Royal had parlayed his savings into land holdings. He began cattle ranching and over time his ranch and his herd grew. When the American civil war broke out Royal was in an enviable position. The demand was so great he traveled to Mexico to buy more cattle in Tamaulipas and Veracruz. In one village he bought all the cattle in the area. When he realized this would put most of the local *vaqueros* out of work he made them an offer. If they would relocate to his ranch he would help them build homes for their families and provide a good living in return for their work on the ranch and raising the cattle. Nearly all of them agreed and their descendants have lived there since and have a fierce loyalty to the Royal family and the Rancho Royal. They are known as the *Royalistas*.

The South needed his hides and his beef and he made the veritable killing selling his wares for gold currency. He would not accept Confederate money or notes.

The end of the war brought a union occupation and the coming of more extensive railroads. All of these things worked in Royal's favor. Texas returned to the union in 1870 and he continued as before but now supplying the United States army which was now fighting Indians and the growing demand on the east coast and other parts of America.

Royal helped found a small town near the entrance to his ranch and here he backed a new bank, several businesses, a stage coach station and a school. The town was, of course, christened Royalville.

Rancho Royal prospered and grew and following the civil war he continued selling to the U.S. Army and aiding the growing westward movement.

There was a thread of violence woven throughout this story. Royal was known as a hard man with a quick temper. He had to fight Comanches, Kiowas, Lipan and Mescalero Apaches along with Mexican *banditos*, American outlaws and assorted rustlers and thieves to protect his growing empire and he backed down from none. Indeed, he obtained a reputation for ruthlessness. Allegations were there in some accounts of Royal using questionable legal tactics and veiled threats of violence to take over land from Mexican *rancheros* whose deeds dated to royal Spanish land grants from the 18th century.

He embarked on a mostly successful effort to obtain most of the smaller ranches that lay adjacent or near his property and the size of Rancho Royal grew exponentially.

At the time of his death he had built one of the largest cattle empires ever in the history of Texas. His two sons, Lamar and Bowie, inherited equal shares of ownership and administered the business until their deaths. Bowie's daughter was Henrietta, who was now the principal owner and ranch operator. Henrietta had married a Mr. Jacob Caderwaller, a cowboy who had demonstrated much ability with ranching as well as business. He had not been a good match however, falling prey to drink and

11

indolence following his marriage into the leading local family. Henrietta kept her name and her money, divorcing Caderwaller after their son had achieved adulthood. Her son Jacob had married and produced a son Richard II. Richard was orphaned following an accident at sea drowning his parents. Young Richard was now the apple of his grandmother's eye and heir apparent to the vast estate.

"My goodness, Holmes! What have we gotten ourselves into?"

"Very deep waters I suspect," he replied.

"Well, Holmes, I think we need a good meal to fortify ourselves for our first day at sea tomorrow. What do you say to a stop at the restaurant the cabbie told us about?"

"I say, that's a capital idea Watson, let's be off!"

So we ventured out to the restaurant, The Captain's Table, where we enjoyed a substantial meal of beef Wellington garnished by salmon roe on toast. There were English muffins for desert and we washed it down with a carafe of fine Cabernet Sauvignon.

Following our meal we retired early and slept well.

Chapter 5 *Departure*

We awoke the morning early and downed a fast breakfast and coffee before we gathered our bags and headed to the dock to board the *Stephen F. Austin*. The weather had shown a marked improvement and a bright, crisp sky reached endlessly overhead. The docks were already alive with activity as numerous vessels prepared to take advantage of the excellent conditions. Soon we were at the gangway and committed our luggage to the care of the dock master who ensured they were loaded aboard the vessel. We signed the ship's passenger log, handed over our boarding passes and somewhat unsteadily made our way up the gangway to step on board the vessel.

Both Holmes and I had traveled abroad on sea going vessels so this was not an entirely unknown world to us but we were both impressed with the orderly and efficient appearance of the ship and its crew.

We were quickly greeted by Captain Johansen. "Welcome aboard gentlemen! I will have you shown to your quarters and I trust you will be comfortable."

A young seaman appeared and escorted us below to our cabin and there we found our bags were already in place. We made sure all was "ship shape" and went top side to watch the departure.

A ships mate with a brass megaphone began calling out "All ashore who's going ashore," and with that the mooring lines were cast off and the two harbor tugboats, which were lashed to the starboard side of the ship, began to move and we pulled away from the dock. The tugs positioned us into the ship channel and then they cast off their lines and the *Stephen F. Austin* began to move, slowly, under its own power. We stood along the rail on the after deck and soon the port fell behind us and we approached the end of the channel and the open sea.

A group of dolphins appeared suddenly and began riding the wake of the ship's bow and we delighted in their seeming exuberance as they sped alongside the ship. Among them we saw a few youngsters swimming excitedly with their parents.

In what seemed no time at all we cleared the jetties and ventured out into the Atlantic Ocean. The weather was, as I had mentioned, exceptional and the seas were running lightly. We could not have asked for a more pleasant experience up to this point.

We found two deck chairs and seated ourselves and wrapped up in blankets as we marveled at the sight of the vast expanse of ocean as the land fell away behind us. The purser brought us some hot coffee and crumpets and we indulged ourselves with the complete enjoyment of the experience. The ship rode the light seas well and soon was up to speed. Now we were truly out at sea.

Chapter 6 *Atlantic Crossing*

On our first night out we were honored to have the captain invite us to eat dinner at the officer's mess. We were seated at the table and a Filipino steward provided us water and menus. There were a few other passengers at the table as well as Captain Johansen and his mates.

Captain Johansen began the conversation. "Let me welcome you all to the *Stephen F. Austin*. I anticipate a pleasant and rapid crossing. The weather seems in our favor and I trust you will all enjoy the experience."

At this point introductions were made. All but one was from Texas. Seated with us was a middle aged couple, Mr. and Mrs. Albert Whitman, from New Braunfels, Mr. Juan Gonzales, from San Antonio, Mr. Stuart Walker, also from San Antonio and an attractive young couple, Mr. and Mrs. Morley Draper from Houston. Mr. Gustav Mueller was from Germany and he spoke flawless English.

Following dinner and small talk Captain Johansen produced a box of cigars for those who desired them and he offered Brandy.

I took a cigar, a fine Cuban smoke, as did Holmes. We both also took a brandy.

"I suggest we all tell a little about ourselves. I am Captain Bernard Johansen of New Bedford, Massachusetts. I have spent my life at sea, starting as an able bodied seaman and plying the trade until I became a captain. I have circumnavigated the globe and made many Atlantic crossings."

The Whitmans had been in Europe visiting relatives in Germany. Mr. Whitman owned several dry goods stores in the Texas Hill Country. Gonzales was returning from Spain following a business trip concerning his import company which helped supply stores such as the Whitman's. He had a business connection with them. Mr. Walker was an attorney working primarily in the field of business and some immigration issues. The Drapers had been Honeymooning in Paris and Switzerland. Mr. Mueller was in the distillery business and provided expertise and equipment to new breweries which were springing up in Texas and Mexico.

When it fell to me to speak I gave my name and started to say that Holmes and I were on a trip to investigate a mystery when Holmes gave me a sharp look and jabbed me with his foot beneath the table. He obviously did not want our purpose revealed. So I just said "My friend Holmes and I want to see the south west for ourselves." Holmes simply described himself as a "consultant, on holiday."

Following our very pleasant dinner we retired to our cabin. We each had our own comfortable armchair and as we smoked Holmes had a question.

"So, Watson, what did you think of our traveling companions?"

"Well, they seem a very nice group, prosperous and well educated. I can't say anything was particularly striking."

"Nor can I, "said Holmes. "Walker impresses me as a man of action and resolve. However I suspect that all of them must have some connection with Rancho Royal or else they would not likely be on this voyage. I do not yet know if that is so; it's just a supposition on my part."

"Well that does make some sense." I replied.

"Indeed!"

Over the course of the next few days we spent most of the time talking our exercise by walking the decks. We spent a good amount of time napping in our deck chairs and Capitan Johansen was good enough to offer us a tour of the ship where we visited the engine room and the boilers, the wireless shack where the telegraph was located, the galley, the steering compartment below deck and all of the areas of interest. I found most interesting the tour of the bridge, where the captain and the helmsman operated the ship. It commanded a good view of the forward areas and of the seas ahead. It also featured a weather station with gauges such as a barometer, wind speed and direction indicators, a thermometer for sea and air temperatures.

After a few days we fell into a pattern and most of our waking time was spent at cards with Walker, Mueller and Gonzales. The couples kept mostly to themselves.

Walker had a keen intellect and made excellent conversation. Gonzales had a fair command of English and seemed a fine fellow. Mueller was a bit harder to get a read on. He was a bit gruff and abrupt in his social skills and seemed out of sorts or impatient most of the time. He also cheated at cards.

On one occasion Walker, Mueller and Gonzales and I were playing a four handed game of five card draw, poker was the favored game on this cruise, Holmes was a quiet observer.

Suddenly Walker reached out a grabbed hold of Mueller's right wrist. "Take your hand off of me!" Mueller snarled.

"Not until you turn tour hand over and show me the card you just slipped from your sleeve!" said Walker forcefully.

"How dare you!" Mueller sputtered.

Walker had a firm grasp and forced Mueller's hand. Out came an ace of spades which Mueller had rather clumsily tried to palm.

"You know Mr. Mueller that could get you killed in some of the places I learned to play poker."

Mueller stood up quickly, his face crimson, his expiration coming in great snorts.

The group of us looked on in silent astonishment as Mueller stalked away.

"Well gentlemen, it seems that Mr. Mueller is *not* a gentleman!" said Walker.

Following that episode Mueller kept to his cabin and we did not see him again until the end of the voyage.

Chapter 7 *Crossing continues…*

Our voyage went so smoothly I began, in my imagination, to fancy my life as it might have been as a seaman, making a living sailing the globe. Of course my fantasy focused on beautiful weather and a girl in every port and omitted the periodic instances of storms and shipwrecks!

I spent most of the daylight hours walking the deck gazing out sea and joining Holmes on the quarter deck snoozing in a lounge chair. After an initial period of interest Holmes had seemingly become bored with the sea and spent what seemed an inordinate amount of time sleeping!

We continued to dine with the little group that had formed early on in the voyage. Reading all the material we had obtained from Mr. Taylor took a several days. We then just relaxed and enjoyed the cruise.

"What are your thoughts so far Holmes?" I asked.

"We don't yet have the real pertinent facts. We cannot even conjecture until we meet Mrs. Royal and find out exactly what she wants us to do Watson. All in all it's very strange, that someone would go to the extreme of hiring us, leasing a ship and still not telling us very much about the case. Very strange indeed," said a reflective Holmes.

Though Holmes gave the impression of being bored and uninterested on the ship I knew full well he was observing and thinking all the while. He was like a cat lying in wait for a mouse.

The weather still held and in a little over a week we were in part of the Atlantic near Bermuda which we passed too far to give us a glimpse of the island.

On a visit to the bridge Captain Johansen told us he was pleased with our progress so far.

"Yes, gentlemen, this has obviously been a smooth trip. It won't be too long before we will enter the Caribbean Sea," said the captain.

He informed us we would round the Florida peninsula and make a call in New Orleans where he planned to refuel, pick up stores, load and offload some cargo.

There we will be switching ships to a shallow draft coastal steamer which will take us to Corpus Christi Bay through Aransas Pass.

We might normally put in at Galveston but that poor island city was devastated a few years ago in a mighty hurricane.

"It will be some time, if ever, they recover from such a disaster," said the captain.

"Yes, I heard about that," said Holmes. "I recall something to the effect that estimates of the dead ranged from 5,000 to 10,000 souls lost in the storm; none will ever know the true toll."

"That's correct Mr. Holmes," Said Captain Johansen. "I saw the devastation not long after the storm. It was like a scene from Armageddon."

"Well Watson, I for one am looking forward to a visit to New Orleans! I have heard much about the place and knowing of your appreciation for fine food and libations I am sure you will enjoy the cuisine and ambience!

"I understand accommodations are waiting for you in New Orleans, "said Johansen.

Chapter 8 *Port of New Orleans*

Soon the *Stephen F. Austin* rounded the Florida peninsula and we made our passage through the Keys. We were now in the Gulf of Mexico. Still the weather held and we had a south east wind which created light seas and at our backs making our transit a smooth one.

That evening after supper Holmes produced a colorful poster advertising the Creole Club in New Orleans. The entertainer featured was one with the colorful sobriquet of Jelly Roll Morton.

"Captain Johansen gave me this Watson. It was on the wall in his cabin. I would like to see this man play piano while we are in New Orleans. He is a large player in the new music style known as "jazz."

"You mean that cacophonous noise I sometimes hear you playing on your gramophone?" I asked.

"Yes Watson. That music is the emergence of an entirely new art form I believe."

"Harrumph! Well I suppose we will have a night or two before we resume our voyage westward."

The weather underwent a drastic change the next morning shortly after sunrise. The winds had shifted suddenly from the north and the temperature had dropped significantly. The skies had seen building clouds the previous day but now were blown clear by this strong weather event.

"Nothing to worry about," said the first mate on his rounds. "This is common this time of year. Sometimes these "northers" are very strong but this seems like a relatively mild one," he reassured us. "It shouldn't affect our schedule and we should be docked by tomorrow morning.

We went to the rail and watched as the seas were whipped to windblown peaks with spray flying from the crests. An Unpleasant queasiness welled inside of me as. For the first time on the voyage, I felt a twinge of sea sickness. Holmes seemed unaffected at first but after a short time he asked his leave for a moment and walked away to a spot on the rail and I saw him leaning out over the rail. I averted my eyes not wishing to witness Holmes in his moment of illness.

I had enjoyed the long sea voyage but I was looking forward to getting back on *terra firma*. I had wanted to witness our entry into the mouth of the Mississippi River but it was well past my bedtime when that event was to occur but I still felt a bit "green" still so I decided to turn in and miss that moment.

When we awoke the new day we found ourselves sailing up the river known as "The Father of Waters." The river was vast and we saw along the banks near pristine marshlands dotted with small islands and patches of water as far as we could see. Everywhere we beheld sea birds of all types. Gulls, egrets, and giant blue herons were most numerous but there were also roseate spoonbills, a magnificent bird, cranes and what I took to be an osprey sitting on a rare tree top. Most of the land was covered with a type of salt grass. It seemed to be the world of eons past when land and life emerged from the waters.

"Look Holmes!" I shouted and pointed to a group of very large crocodilians basking on the bank with their huge jaws agape.

"Yes Watson, alligators! I understand they are common on this coast and especially here in Louisiana."

This sighting further enhanced my impression of a primordial landscape.

Chapter 9 *The Big Easy*

We awoke to find our vessel tied up to the dock. We quickly packed our bags and set them on the cabin floor as we headed to the dining area for a quick bite of breakfast and some coffee.

Here we said our goodbyes to Captain Johansen and our traveling companions.

"Mr. Holmes, Mr. Watson, it was a pleasure to have you with us. There is a gentleman, a Mr. Ortega, waiting to aid you with your needs onshore. Goodbye and good luck gentlemen."

I thanked the captain, "Our compliments Captain Johansen."

Holmes and I shook hands with the captain and headed down the gangway to the dock.

We caught sight of a man holding a sign that read; "Sherlock Holmes, Dr. Watson."

"Mr. Ortega, I presume?" said Holmes as we approached the man.

"*Si señor*. Welcome to the United States."

Ortega shook hands with us most vigorously. He was a tall, well-built Latin man and seemed very friendly.

"I am Domingo Ortega. I work for *Señora* Royal here in New Orleans."

Holmes and I introduced ourselves as he guided us to a waiting carriage with our bags loaded on the back.

"We have reserved rooms for you at Hotel Saint Louis on Bienville Street, off Canal Street. It is very nice." Ortega then motioned towards a nearby open carriage "Here *señores*, I have arranged transportation."

So Holmes and I trundled into the carriage and rolled down the docks and into the great city. Here we were presented with a spectacle I would not have imagined. The place was alive with activity and everywhere people were walking, riding in carriages and coaches, riding horseback and loaded into wagons. The street lights were bright and cafes, restaurants, hotels, saloons, clubs and yes, houses of ill repute openly offering their wares.

"What a place Watson!" exclaimed Holmes. "A gentleman could lose himself for a while in a place like this."

Street musicians claimed corners and patches of roadside and serenaded passersby hoping for a monetary show of appreciation. We observed a large number of Negroes and others of mixed race interacting freely with whites as if this was the normal practice.
"It doesn't seem as if "Jim Crow" has the same influence here as I have heard about other parts of the south," observed Holmes. We had read about the Jim Crow laws which were passed by southern legislatures in the years following the War Between the States to diminish the voting power and the integration into society by freed blacks.

Soon we had been checked into our very nice hotel. The Hotel Saint Louis featured beautiful French colonial architecture and an extravagant opulence worthy of the robber barons. Our rooms were excellent and provided a nice view from the balcony of the hustle and bustle alive in the streets below. Ortega said he would meet us in the lobby and we would have dinner together and make plans for the rest of the trip.

Chapter 10 *An Evening In New Orleans*

As he had said he would Ortega was waiting in the lobby.

"*Buenas noches señores.*" Ortega guided us to an open carriage.

"Mr. Ortega, are you familiar with the Creole Club? We desire to take in the entertainment there this evening," said Holmes.

"Yes. I know the place. The ride will be a short one and you will get a nice view of Canal Street and part of the French Quarter," replied Ortega.

Once again we were thrust into the sights and sounds of New Orleans and the raw energy the place seemed to generate. Soon were arrived at our destination and found ourselves a table near the front which offered a good view of the piano stand. As of the moment the piano was unattended.

"What is your pleasure *señores*? Mrs. Royal has instructed me to look after your needs while here in New Orleans," said a broadly smiling Ortega.

Holmes ordered a whiskey and I followed suit. Ortega had rum and soda with a lime. The very attractive waitress served our drinks.

"My guess is this is Kentucky bourbon," I said after a sip. "And very good too. It goes down very smoothly." Holmes agreed.

"Yes gentlemen. Here in New Orleans we go very much for the finer things in life."

The club certainly testified to that sentiment. It was plush and lavishly decorated with a full serving staff and full liquor cabinets behind the several bars in the place.

A well-dressed man with the bearing of a circus ringmaster had made his way to the piano stand. With a ringmaster's voice he bellowed "Ladies and gentlemen! Please welcome to the bandstand the rising star of the Crescent City Mr. Jelly Roll Morton!"

A slim man of average height and of mixed race strode out from the wings, very proudly I would say, and seated himself at the piano. He said nothing to the club goers and immediately began playing the piano. His music was energetic and, to my ears, rather unconventional with a driving rhythm and somewhat percussive quality.

I glanced at Holmes; he had a rapturous look on his face.

"This man is breaking new territory Watson, he will be long remembered I wager."

"If you say so Holmes." I was not convinced but I admit my musical appreciation is limited.

"How about a short walk before we return to the hotel Watson?"

"That sounds good Holmes. We can take in the sights and smoke a cigar," I replied.

"Ortega, could you serve as our guide?"

"Of course," replied Ortega.

We enjoyed the walk in this vibrant city and enjoyed the variety of humanity we observed here. As we neared the hotel a tall, very distinguished black man approached us. He was wearing a top hat and tails with a bright red vest.

"Gentleman, a word," he said as he approached us. He had some sort of Caribbean accent I could not pin point.

"Yes?" Holmes said to the man.

"I see you have come a long way and are on a great quest. You have traveled far," He said.

"And how have you arrived at that conclusion?" asked Holmes.

"Sirs, I can see by your dress and by your speech that y'all aint from around here," he replied. "I would say, you gentleman hail from England. Also I see that you display an alertness and intensity that demonstrates you are not on a sight-seeing trip."

"A man after my own heart Watson!"

I have something that will help you," he said in his deep, resonant voice.

"What might that be sir?" asked Holmes.

He reached into his inside coat pocket and produced a small leather bag and some strange looking, organic thing which I could not identify.

"This is John the Conqueroo," he said as he held up the small unknown object. "And this is a mojo bag."

A puzzled Holmes asked "And what, pray tell are those?"

"This is the root of the Saint John's Wort. I place it into the mojo bag and I cast a spell over it. It will give you great power and protection. I ask only a small consideration," he replied.

"How much of a consideration?" asked Holmes.

"Only twenty dollars for such power and it is yours."

"Very well," replied Holmes. "It so happens we are well heeled at the moment!" Holmes had a small supply of American currency and gave him the money.

The man took it, thanked us and was suddenly gone down the street.

"Well, Watson! A little New Orleans hoodoo! What a novelty aye?"

"That was quite a large sum Holmes!"

"Yes but he intrigued my interest. Someday I would like to spend some time here. Come, let's return to the hotel."

So after an enjoyable evening we turned in.

The next day we spent again studying materials on the Royal Ranch and the geography of the Gulf Coast. Ortega brought us boarding passes for the coastal steamer *San Jacinto* which we would be boarding in the morning. He also handed us an envelope containing $1,000 American dollars. "For expenses," he said.

"Mrs. Royal is most generous!" exclaimed Holmes.

The following morning dawned clear, cool and windy as a north wind blew out to sea. We had our breakfast and Ortega escorted us back to the docks where we boarded our second ship, the small coastal steamer the *SS San Jacinto*.

Soon we were underway and out into the Gulf of Mexico bound for Corpus Christi. The ship's captain, Captain James Donleavey, introduced himself, and welcomed us aboard. He said our voyage would be two days and one night in duration. Our quarters were much smaller and spartan on this ship but comfortably adequate. The galley served up a simple but hearty fare and as the captain said we arrived off the Aransas Pass on schedule. Here we anchored and waited. This pass through the barrier islands was notorious for its shifting sand bars on which many vessels had wrecked or run aground over the years.

Captain Donleavey informed us that we would sail into port in the morning upon the high tide and the arrival of the pilot. Here we would, once more, meet a representative of Mrs. Royal with our transportation and any further instructions.

After a comfortable night swinging at anchor we once again felt the boat moving.

"The pilot must be here Watson, it seems we are underway!"

Chapter 11 *Port of Corpus Christi*

Holmes and I went up to the deck to see what we could. As we approached shore we could make out a low lying beach, a small village and soon we approached the infamous Aransas Pass which was marked by a two long granite jetties on either side.

Our extraordinary luck concerning rough seas held as we crossed the bar and only encountered a light swell. We emerged from the pass into a large bay and wetlands area. We were in a channel which had been dredged and was used for ship traffic.

We followed this channel for some distance. The wetland areas much resembled the scene we had encountered as we saw approaching New Orleans. Eventually the channel made a slow left hand turn and we emerged into Corpus Christi Bay, a large circular, shallow body of water. Soon the town and its waterfront came in sight.

There were two very long piers extending well out into the bay. Soon we docked at one of them.

We gathered our luggage, bade our good byes and walked down the gangway. Once again we were met by a man who approached us.

"Mr. Holmes? Dr. Watson I presume?"

We acknowledged our identities.

"I am Manuel Garcia, I work for *Señora* Royal. Happy to meet you."

"Our regards," said Holmes. "We are looking forward to arriving soon at Rancho Royal after our long journey."

"I am sure you are. I have made arrangements for you here and if you need to stay a few days to rest that is fine," said Garcia.

"I believe would very much like to get underway in the morning if that is possible," said Holmes.

"Certainly *señor*," replied Garcia. "I will see all is in readiness for tomorrow morning."

Our gear was loaded onto a flat car with benches pulled by a small steam operated tractor, it was called a steam mule. A narrow gauge set of railroad tracks ran the length of the pier. The need for such a long pier was necessitated by the shallowness of the bay which didn't allow larger vessels close to shore. As we neared the end of the pier we saw a wharf close by covered with stacks of cotton bales waiting to be shipped.

Garcia had a wagon waiting, it was an open, flat bed affair with no sides but had two benches for passengers. He called it a buckboard. Our things were loaded on board and we rode into town.

Corpus Christi was a small town but had an air of prosperity as we observed large Victorian style homes built upon a bluff overlooking the waterfront. The street we rode upon was constructed of crushed sea shells compacted into a road bed. Some streets were unpaved and we saw others paved with macadam.

The buckboard took us to a large hotel, the Hotel Saint Louis. We checked in and relaxed a bit. The accommodations were just adequate.

"Well Watson, here we are in Texas!" Holmes seemed somewhat amused.

Chapter 12 *Overnight In Corpus Christi, Departure For Rancho Royal*

After a too brief nap, we freshened up and joined Garcia who had sent us a message from the lobby.

"*Buenas noches señores!*" Garcia seemed in an ebullient mood. "I trust you are refreshed and ready for some dinner? I know just the place. I will wager you are not familiar with Mexican food?"

"Quite correct," said Holmes. "I have the feeling that is soon to change."

Garcia led us a short distance down the street to a place emblazoned with a large sign reading "*Taqueria Jalisco*". It was a non-descript wood

frame building with wooden floors. We took a table and a very attractive, dark eyed young woman brought us menus and glasses of water.

"Garcia, we are in your hands here. Please order something for us," I said.

"With pleasure *señores!*" He spoke to the waitress in Spanish. He then asked if we would like beer before the meal and if we liked spicy food. Holmes once again said we were in his hands.

"When it comes to Mexican food we are babes in the woods!" said Holmes.

Soon the waitress returned with a tray and set before us bottles of beer, *Dos Equis*, from Mexico. She also had a small basket full of corn chips and a beautiful small pottery dish containing some kind of red sauce.

"This is *salsa*. Dip your chip into it and scoop some up. I think you will like it," said Garcia.

Garcia demonstrated by taking a chip and scooping up a liberal amount of the salsa and eating the whole thing in one bite. He followed it with a drink of his beer and a slice of lime which he placed to his lips.

Holmes and I followed suit. It was tasty enough but almost instantly I felt my forehead breaking out with little beads of sweat and my mouth and tongue rebelled against the sudden surge of heat! I reached for the water immediately.

"Good god man!" I was drinking more water rapidly. "That set me on fire!"

Holmes laughed saying nothing but I noticed his own forehead had the same beads of sweat! He took a very big gulp from his beer!

Our food was brought to the table with a warning that the plates were very hot. Our dinner consisted of some strange items to us which Garcia described as *tamales*, *enchiladas* and a *tostada*. Beans and rice were the side dishes. A small silver bowl with a domed top was placed on the center of the table along with a dish of butter. I lifted the top and a small cloud of steam rose up revealing a pile of flat, disc shaped objects made of crushed corn which were called *tortillas*. Garcia said this was a typical Mexican dinner and these were very popular selections. He told us to slather a bit of the salsa on the food. I was not sure about that advice and was very stingy with the salsa.

"Try these," said Garcia as he passed a bowl containing some fat, green oval shaped peppers. "*Jalapeños*, he said.

I took a bite of one particularly shiny, chubby little pepper and I instantly thought my mouth was going to melt from the heat. "Goodness gracious!" I reached for my water glass quickly emptying it. The sweat was now breaking out on the back of my neck!

Garcia chuckled and said "You probably should never try the *Habanero* peppers!"

Overall I liked the food, even with the ordeal by fire, and I think Holmes did as well though he said little. I noticed he did have another beer following dinner and he drank it rapidly!

Garcia said there would be a coach ready for us in the morning to take us to the rail terminal for the Tex-Mex Railway where we would take a train on to the Rancho Royal.

Chapter 13 *Rancho Royal*

We were taken to the terminal for the Tex-Mex Railway. Here we found a rather small train pulled by a Whitcombe locomotive and consisting of two flat cars loaded with farming machinery, two boxcars and two passenger cars. Garcia had our luggage loaded on and he accompanied us into the passenger car. I took a window seat.

Soon we were rolling and left Corpus Christi behind. I gazed out the window and lit a cigar. The land rolling by my window was flat, dry grassland surrounded by a barbed wire fence. Here and there clumps of gnarled trees and prickly pear cactus were scattered amongst grazing cattle. We passed acres of farmland, now under the plow and being readied for next year's planting. Cotton and sorghum were the biggest crops here we were told. It wasn't long before we came to the town of Royalville. We passed on through the small town and again we were out in the surrounding ranch lands.

After a while we came to a break in the fence to allow the train cars to pass. A large sign posted on the fence read "Rancho Royal, Trespassers Will Be Shot!"

Soon thereafter we came to a loading dock and warehouse; here we came to a stop.

"Here we are," said Garcia as he ushered us out of the car and to another buckboard. We and our gear were trundled aboard and we were soon underway. We were taken to a complex of assorted buildings. As we drew near we discerned a large home, somewhat resembling a Victorian style home, with three stories and a covered porch running around all sides. It was in most respects a conventional home except for the walls which seemed to be constructed from some sort of earthen brick. We would find out these were *adobe* bricks, made right here on the ranch. Large willows, pecan and cottonwood trees provided shade on the porch and the home itself.

"One moment and I will see if *Señora* Royal is home now," said Garcia as he slipped to the ground and made his way into the house. Shortly he returned to tell us to make ourselves comfortable in the drawing room as Mrs. Royal was on her way to the house now.

"Thank you," said Holmes, "But I would prefer to wait here on the porch if you don't mind. The air is cool and the breeze is fresh and it is most pleasant in the shade."

"As you wish *señor*. Just let me know if there is anything you require."

We sat there very comfortably and relaxed. We asked for some tea which was promptly produced.

Shortly we heard some kind of commotion and saw a large cloud of dust approaching rapidly. As it approached we could make out several figures on horseback and we could hear the hooves of the galloping horses and hear the cries of men, "*Arriba! Andale! Vamonos muchachos!*"

Three riders peeled off out of the bunch and approached the house. They quickly dismounted and tied their horses' reins to a rail in front of the fence.

As they approached we could see one was a woman. She walked towards us as we descended from the porch to meet her.

"Mr. Holmes? Doctor Watson? I am Mrs. Royal," she extended her right hand. Mrs. Royal was a tall, thin woman who seemed very fit and tan though her white hair, which was mostly tucked up into her Spanish style flat brimmed black hat, belied her age. Her hat had a black band adorned with small, silver conchos, a sort of dish like jewelry. She wore a waist coat and trousers, all black and a white shirt beneath the waistcoat. Her jacket and trousers had floral patterned embroidery unobtrusively placed around the waist and on the pants legs.

"It is a pleasure to finally meet you gentlemen."

Holmes responded "Indeed it is so for us as well. It was a long journey to get here."

Holmes took her hand, without much enthusiasm it seemed. "I am Sherlock Holmes and yes, this is my esteemed colleague Dr. Watson," said Holmes with a barely perceivable nod of his head. I too shook hands but said nothing for the moment.

"I have been eager to finally meet you," said Mrs. Royal. We will get you comfortably installed in your rooms and I will lay out the whole business over dinner. I imagine you have some questions."

Chapter 14 *Inside the Ranch House*

Quickly we all entered the house. Some of her *vaqueros* transported our luggage to our rooms on the ground floor.

We got a good look at the interior as we walked through a foyer and into the drawing room.

What they called the living room was a large place with a high ceiling with exposed rafters and beams. Wood paneling adorned the walls punctuated by a baroque patterned red and black wall paper. There were mirrors and paintings distributed around the circumference of the room and the heads of many unfortunate wild beasts were hung helter skelter along the interior. Our bedrooms were on the ground floor near the back of the house. Our rooms were comfortable and well lighted and each featured a four poster bed, sumptuously made with goose feather filled mattresses!

The lighting was good and came through large double windows with shutters opened. A small writing desk complete with chair was also in each room. We were informed that dinner would be served at 5:30 and we were expected to be prompt! Holmes and I decided to use this brief interim to take a nap and catch up on some much needed sleep.

In what seemed no time at all were awakened by a rap on the door and some disembodied voice told us dinner would be served in fifteen minutes. We scrambled to freshen a bit and comb our hair and soon we were entering the dining room. We were seated at a long table with Mrs. Royal, in a respectable but modest black evening dress, at the head Holmes and I as the only guests. Our meal was excellent and consisted of oysters on the half shell as appetizers and very tender barbecued brisket and sausage with potato salad and red beans. This was novel fare for us.

"Excellent!" Holmes said. He said he was a confirmed beef eater and he thoroughly enjoyed his meal. I seconded the motion and we washed down the meal with some excellent red wine.

"Well, now we are together and we can get down to business," said Mrs. Royal.

"Yes Mrs. Royal, I think we need all the facts and we need to know just what it is that you want us to do," said Holmes.

Chapter 15 *The Case Is Made*

We retired as a group into the drawing room and took comfortable seats and another glass of the fine wine.

"Well Mr. Holmes," said Mrs. Royal, "Here is the case."

"My grandson Richard has disappeared. He has been missing for over three months now. I first reported him missing to the local sheriff's department but their investigations proved fruitless. The Texas Rangers were called in but they, too, drew a blank. I have had teams of my *vaqueros* sweeping the ranch since he went missing but nothing has turned up."

"Tell me about your grandson please," said a somber, respectful Holmes.

"Richard is a fine young man. He has a good character, he is well educated, handsome and he was brought up here to learn all aspects of the ranch and the business. He has a great future and as my sole heir stands to inherit a great estate with many responsibilities."

"Was Richard happy here Mrs. Royal?" queried Holmes in a low voice.

"Yes, I think so," she replied. "He loved the ranch, he was a good hand, I have no reason to think he was unhappy."

Holmes walked slowly towards the large window and gazed outside, "Do you suspect foul play or do you think some sort of accident befell him?"

"I have no idea. The day he disappeared he was last seen riding one of his favorite horses out onto the Mendoza trail which leads out into a wild and undeveloped section of the ranch. Richard often rode there because he liked the wild life and the solitude there." Mrs. Royal paused for a sip of wine and continued. "Any way, the day he was last seen he rode off after saying he was going for a ride and would be back for lunch. I did not think much about it at the time."

"How was he dressed?" asked Holmes.

"He was wearing regular work clothes, the norm here really. He had on a broad brimmed felt hat, a loose light blue chambray work shirt, a red bandana, boots, heavy denim pants. Really nothing out of the ordinary."

"Was he armed?" asked Holmes.

"Yes Mr. Holmes. We always go about armed."

"In what manner?" asked Holmes.

"When riding out onto the range Richard always carried a side arm, a Colt .45 revolver, a knife and a Winchester 30/30 repeating rifle," she said. "He also carried a lasso and a bull whip, and he knew how to use them."

"Do go on," said Holmes.

"Well, when he did not return I began to have some concern. My concern intensified when his horse came home without him. Just before dark myself and a small group of *vaqueros* went out to see if we could find him. We picked up his trail but it soon ran out in the rocks and very hard dry ground. Nothing has turned up. We still send out search parties and all of the hands are advised to be on the lookout," said Mrs. Royal.

"What about his accoutrements?"

"His rope, whip and rifle were with the horse when it returned."

"What can you tell me about his personal life? Any friends, enemies, lovers...?" asked Holmes.

"We..., he has only a few friends living as we do far from town. I knew of no enemies and he did have a couple of girlfriends while he was in college but here he kept his head down and was totally immersed in his work. He never complained and always seemed a happy young man."

"I should like to see the trail where was last seen. Also I would like to look over the ranch, see something of the operations and talk to some of the workers," said Holmes. "Do you have a recent photograph of the young man?"

"Yes, here it is. You may keep this." She produced an 8x10 photograph of a handsome, smiling young man.

"Mr. Holmes, you have *carte blanche* to proceed as you deem necessary. Just let me know what I can do to help you," said Mrs. Royal. "You two may go by the store and get yourself some proper attire for riding out in the brush."

Holmes made a slight nod of his head. "Thank you."

Chapter 16 *We Go Out Into The Bush*

We were taken to the general store where we could select some clothing for out outdoor investigations. The store was a fantastic place filled with clothing, boots, hats, guns, belts, saddles and all imaginable types of items one would require for work and leisure here on the ranch. The store manager, Hilario Fuentes, told us the ranch had its own saddle and leather shop, a necessity for such an operation as Rancho Royal.

We selected our ranch wear and retired to our room to change. Holmes had chosen a flat brimmed Spanish style hat, black denims and an attractive light blue western style shirt. I had picked a large sombrero style cowboy hat, a white shirt, a red bandana, denims and a pair of leather chaps which I was told would offer protection from thorns and sharp sticks while riding in the brush country. We were a sight to behold!

A knock on our door heralded the arrival of our boots which had been saddled soaped and "worked" to soften and water proof the leather. We slid them on, with some difficulty.

"I say Holmes these boots are rather tight!" I wasn't so sure I wanted to change my footwear.

"You're right Watson. I suspect a bit of wear will him break them in," replied Holmes.

I am sure that even Holmes felt a bit embarrassed by the strange spectacle we must have presented with our appearance!

We went outside and there we encountered a cowboy with three large horses.

"Howdy boys!" bellowed the large man with the horses. "I am Connor Lovejoy, ranch foreman. "I wanted to get you and the horses used to each other and show you around" He stuck out a large right hand and vigorously shook our hands.

"Have you boys done any riding before?"

"Why yes," I replied. "Both Holmes and myself have some experience. However our tack and saddles are quite different!"

"No problem, you will get used to western style real quick like. This here is Lilly and this is Pancho. They are good riding horses and are very forgiving. I will let you all get to know each other and you can pick your horse."

I happened to be standing next to Lilly, a large grey mare with some dappled spots on her posterior. She made eye contact with me and licked me on the hand! It was love at first sight.

"It appears that Lilly has made the choice," chuckled Holmes. He climbed up onto the saddle on Pancho and I mounted up on Lilly.

The western saddles were much larger and I would say more comfortable than our English riding saddles. The leather work was exquisite and we were quite excited to be in our western garb, on horseback, here on one of the largest cattle ranches in the world. Who would have ever believed it?

The horses were magnificent, well trained and calm, responsive to the slightest touch. The three of us rode off into the sunset, so to speak.

As we rode along Mr. Lovejoy briefed us on what we saw and about the ranch and its many facets.

"As you have seen we have a general store. Here the hands can get whatever they need and it comes out of their pay. We try to be self-reliant here, we have our own church, some priests and nuns. They run a school and a dispensary. We have a post office, a blacksmith and a small library. All of the younger people have learned English, Mrs. Royal places much importance on that."

We came by a *corral*, a large fenced in area where they were branding cattle. We had to stop and see this.

Mr. Lovejoy explained, "These are cows recently brought in from the range and have never been branded."

We watched with great interest as cattle were singled out by cowboys on horseback and guided into a short wooden chute where they passed through and were taken by the head by means of a lasso and hands on. Once in the new enclosure they were roped by the feet, thrown down and another cowboy would have a red hot branding iron, embossed with the Double R brand, which he would press into the cow's flesh, searing hair, skin and all with the brand. The cow would bellow for a while but the entire operation took only a few minutes until the cow, startled but not injured, would amble off into its herd. It seemed none the worse for the experience and seemed to get over it all rather quickly.

We rode across some pastures where cattle in large numbers grazed. The cattle here were large, beefy creatures unlike any I had ever encountered,

Seeming to read my thoughts Mr. Lovejoy interjected "These cows are our own line, developed for the meat market. We crossed several breeds to develop this line which we think will be very profitable. We call them "Santa Maria" Cattle.

In another pasture we saw examples of breeds we didn't have to ask the names. Here were Long Horns and two big, red and wooly Highland Coos! (cows)

"Highland Coos! Why I haven't seen any of these in years! As a boy I knew a man that raised these lovely beasts."

"I am glad you like them Dr. Watson. This is Angus and Hamish. We are looking for some mates for them," said Mr. Lovejoy.

Another cowboy rode up to us. Mr. Lovejoy introduced us. "This is Manuel Peralta, he is our best tracker."

"*Mucho gusto*," said Peralta.

We continued on until we came into a large unfenced are. A trail was barely evident as we rode into this brushy area choked with mesquite trees, cactus and sage brush.

"This is the Mendoza trail. It was here Richard Royal was last seen riding off down the trail," said Mr. Lovejoy.

We quickly left behind all signs of civilization as we entered a totally wild, natural area. Wild life was abundant here. We saw deer sauntering along as if they had no care in the world. Wild turkeys were feeding on the ground and roosting in the branches.

"What, pray tell, are those?" Holmes gestured towards a small group of strange, pig like animals that emerged from a stand of prickly pear cacti.

"*Javelinas*," said Mr. Lovejoy. "They can be mean little critters. We need to give them all the room they need. Their biological name is the collared peccary. They range from here down into the pampas of South America."

One of them approached us and snarled, snapping his jaws with loud clicks and displaying some positively horrifying tusks! As he continued the others of his group calmly disappeared into the grass. He soon followed suit, taking another look back at us and having one last snarling jaw snap.

"Positively unfriendly," I said.

"These animals seem to have no fear of humans," observed Holmes.

"That's true Mr. Holmes. We don't allow hunting here on the ranch except for rare occasions. We enjoy the wildlife and we have some imported animals living here freely as well. Wait till you see one of them big Russian boars we got, and Nilgai from India too. Quite impressive beasts!"

Chapter 17 *Down the Mendoza Trail*

We continued slowly down the trail looking for anything we might use to gain some information. This was a unique experience for us to say the least.

"Recall when we saw Buffalo Bill's Wild West show about twenty years ago at the Earls Court show ground in London? I would never have imagined then we would one day be here seeing it first hand," said I.

"Indeed," said Holmes. "This is fascinating, a fantasy dream come true."

Peralta rode out a little ahead of us. Suddenly he pulled up and quickly dismounted. He walked slowly and then bent down on one knee, picking up something. He produced a cigar butt.

"I know *Sĕnor* Richard must have come this way at some time," said Peralta.

"How do you know that?" Holmes dismounted.

"He smoked these *Cubano* cigars."

"Very good Peralta! A man after my own heart!"

I, too, then dismounted and we walked along the trail and into the adjoining brush. Suddenly a strange sound intruded into my consciousness. The sound was a high pitched, whirring sound. We instinctively froze in our tracks.

"¡*Cuidado*! Don't move." Peralta moved slowly and then stopped again. "Look there."

And there, coiled in a patch of grass adjacent to a stand of prickly pear cactus was a large, thick bodied snake, staring menacingly and shaking its tail with its collection of rattles at an extreme rate.

"A rattlesnake!" exclaimed Holmes. "A western diamondback if I am not mistaken."

"*Si señor*, it will not bother us if we leave him alone. *Vamonos!* Let's move away," said Peralta.

We backed off slowly and led the now somewhat skittish horses a distance. We remounted and once again headed down the trail.

"The snakes are moving slow now. As soon as it gets colder they will go underground till spring. But you still need to watch your step!"

We saw many tracks on the trail, all old and weathered. Apparently many animals used this trail. Presently we came to the banks of a creek. There was water flowing and from the size of the creek bed the water level was low.

"This is Apache Creek," said Peralta.

We easily forded the stream and found no horse tracks on the other side.

"It doesn't seem any horse has been this way lately," said Holmes. "There was no sign of the missing man anywhere?"

"No," replied Peralta.

"Is this stream always so low?" asked Holmes.

"No," said Peralta. "It has gone down lately but for a while it was overflowing because of a large rainstorm."

We dismounted and Holmes made a thorough investigation of the area.

"What are these?" Holmes was pointing to a series of ruts or possible drag marks which appeared all along the banks.

"Those are drag marks from boats as they are pulled ashore or into the water."

"Where does the creek go?" asked Holmes.

It flows into the Laguna Madre, a large body of water running along the coast between the mainland and Padre Island."

"So from here one could potentially reach the open sea?"

"That is correct, it would be possible. There are passes through Padre Island which open out into the Gulf waters," said Peralta.

"Another aspect to consider," mused Holmes reflectively.

Chapter 18 *News*

We returned to the ranch and Peralta took our horses.

"That's a good man Watson. We will likely have use for his assistance later," said Holmes.

We proceeded to the ranch house and took refreshments after brushing off the dust from the trail. Mrs. Royal joined us. She seemed very animated.

"I have news gentlemen. I just received a phone call from the sheriff of Aransas County. They have found a body on the beach of Saint Joseph Island. He thinks it could be my grandson."

She became emotional for a moment but quickly composed herself...

"We will go to the coroner's office there tomorrow. Please come with us. Be prepared to depart very early." With that she withdrew.

We were served our dinner and we settled down in the drawing room for a smoke and a brandy. Holmes seemed pensive and we didn't speak for a while.

"Well Watson," said Holmes. "This could be a very grave turn of events. However it is important we keep an open mind and evaluate the facts as we find them and not be led one way or another by emotion or superficialities."

"What do you mean Holmes?"

"Simply that we first examine the facts, as always, before reaching any conclusions."

"Quite so, quite so," I replied.

With that we retired and the next morning we were awakened by a knock on our door.

"What time is it?" I tried to shake out the cobwebs.

"It is five o'clock in the morning," replied Holmes.

"What an abominable hour to rise!"

A second knock came on our door along with a shout. "Breakfast will be ready in ten minutes gentleman!"

We quickly performed our toilet and pulled on our clothes and made our way to the dining room. After a quick breakfast we met Mrs. Royal and Mr. Lovejoy outside. They had a coach ready with two hands, well-armed, riding on the roof. We boarded in silence and rode to the train dock where a locomotive with a passenger car was waiting. We boarded the small train and quickly made steam and headed east on the tracks.

It was a tense trip with no one speaking and I stared out the window as the passing panorama of an unfamiliar world flashed by.

After a seemingly interminable time we arrived at the train station in Corpus Christi. Here we found a Ford automobile waiting. We boarded the car, as they called it, and quickly passed over the roadway. We came to a narrow and rickety looking wooden bridge over a muddy slough called Hall's Bayou. The ride was rough and I thought a bit precarious but we were carried along until we reached the town of Aransas Pass, on the opposite side of Corpus Christi Bay.

We pulled up in front of the Aransas County Court House, a stately building of a rather *baroque* architecture. We soon found ourselves in the office of the Sherriff's Department and in the presence of a Deputy Bailey.

The deputy led us into a basement room where there was a medical examination station. On a plain white table was the rather ghastly site of a bloated and badly decomposed cadaver. The smell was overwhelming. The face was gone completely with only a grinning skull and a few strips of flesh remaining. The eyes, ears and all soft tissue was gone, some undoubtedly stripped by crabs and other marine life and probably by coyotes as well.

Pieces of clothing were clinging to the corpse and the feet were solidly encased in a pair of very expensive looking boots.

"Oh!" With a loud exhalation Mrs. Royal appeared to collapse but Holmes and I supported her by the arms. "Those are Richard's boots!"

Mrs. Royal, with her handkerchief clamped firmly over her nose and mouth, stared at the corpse for a long while. She then moved closer and walked around and around the dead body, peering very closely.

Particular attention was given to the frozen, skeletal grin of the bare skull. She then motioned to the rest of us to follow as she left the room.

"Mr. Holmes, those are my grandson's clothes and his boots but it is not him"

"You are certain?" Holmes betrayed a note of incredulity in his voice.

"Yes Mr. Holmes. Richard had perfect teeth and this poor creature has two lower molars missing and a chip on another tooth. This is not Richard."

I could see Holmes was impressed with her steel grit and her observation.

"What say you Watson? Is it possible to make a positive identification on such a corpse so long exposed to the rigors of destructive natural elements?"

"It is difficult. I saw many such corpses while serving in Afghanistan and most of those were never identified. However the teeth always remain and if there is a record of any dental work that could go a long way towards making a positive identification."

Holmes walked to the window and took a long gaze. "Then we now have even more of a mystery. It is now obvious we may rule out some of the possibilities concerning accidental death, death by wild animal or any possibility of some mental condition causing him to wander off into the ether. That leaves only kidnapping or willful disappearance on his part."

"So who is this unfortunate soul and how did he come to be thrust into this?" I asked.

"We shall see, Watson, we shall see."

"Mr. Holmes, I reject any notion that Richard might be a party to this. It must, then, be a kidnapping. There can be no other explanation," said Mrs. Royal who was clearly highly agitated at any suggestion that her grandson could be involved in the perpetration of what now seemed a very serious crime.

"Mrs. Royal, I will not entertain any conclusions at the moment in the absence of more facts." Said Holmes in a stern, forthright manner. "Facts! We need facts and not conjecture or, forgive me, conclusions based on emotional attachments."

"As you say Mr. Holmes. You are, of course quite correct. I am in your hands," said Mrs. Royal, who finally gave way to sobs and a severe quaking. Holmes, to my surprise, took her and placed his arm around her as she placed her head on his shoulders and cried freely. "Let us return to the ranch. I must do more work and find out what has been going on in Richard's life over the last months." Holmes whispered softly as our party made our way out of the building to begin our return to the ranch.

Chapter 20 *Casting the net*

The following morning Holmes and I were breakfasting alone and we received a message from Mrs. Royal. Holmes handed to me and asked me to read it out loud, which I did.

"Gentlemen. I am sure you are aware of the difficult and trying day we experienced yesterday. I hope you won't mind if I take a few days off for rest and meditation. I am going to my secluded range house where I might be alone and undisturbed. I will make my return promptly thereafter. Please continue as you see fit and if you need anything my men are ready to help. H. Royal"

"What do you make of this Watson?"

"Well, I would say we have a free rein for a few days," I replied.

"Precisely!" Holmes was emphatic. "We can make good use of this time to talk to people here without their being afraid Mrs. Royal is looking over their backs at every moment."

"Do you think that will make a difference?"

"One never knows what an employee will say when the boss is not present. Think on that," said Holmes.

After breakfast Holmes sent for Peralta and our horses. We once again changed into our cowboy gear. I found it quite exciting!

With Peralta as our guide we took a slow tour around the immediate ranch area.

No one spoke for a while but eventually Holmes turned towards Peralta.

"Did the young Mr. Royal have and friends? Was he close to anyone on the ranch? What about lady admirers?"

Peralta thought a moment then he spoke. "He was close to old De La Vina, a man who once worked and lived on the ranch until he had a dispute with the Royals and he moved off the place."

"Yes? That is interesting," said Holmes. "Can you tell us more?"

Peralta continued. "Well, De la Vina has a beautiful granddaughter and I think *Señor* Richard was very much taken with her."

"Can you take us to see him?"

"Yes but not until I get off work around dark. Meet me outside the gate at seven and I will bring the horses and we will go there."

We met Peralta and followed him away from the ranch. The sun was down leaving only traces of the brilliant red sunset behind. The air was cool but bracing.

"What a lovely evening!" I was soaking in the air, the star studded skies and the novelty of our once again riding out onto the range!

After a lengthy ride, we had left the main road far behind, we came to a lonely cabin and a small shed and corral. Two mules and a horse were feeding at their stalls, a light shone through the cabin windows and a trace of smoke slowly curled up into the sky.

"This is the place," said Peralta as he slid off his horse and bade us to follow. He knocked on the door.

"*¿Quien es?*" came a gruff voice from the interior.

"*¡Soy yo! Manuel. Tengo dos amigos que quieren encontrarte.*"

"*Venga,*" Was the answer.

We entered the rather crude domicile and there we met the resident.

"I am Diego De La Vina, at your service gentleman. Please take a seat," He motioned to two chairs and a stool. "Manuel, would you pour some of my special brandy?"

We took our seats and sipped our drinks slowly. The place was cozy and colorful weavings and dried flowers adorned the walls. A nice fire burned in the small hearth. The furniture was wooden and painted in colorful hues. A large dog lay motionless beside his master but his gaze was on us.

De La Vina laughed and said "This is *Lobo*! He must like you, he didn't move a muscle!"

Chapter 21 *Don Diego*

"So, Gentlemen, what is it I can do for you?"

Peralta introduced us. "Don Diego, these two men are here seeking to find out what happened to *Señor* Ricardo. This is *Señor* Holmes and *Señor* Watson. They wanted to talk to you and see what they might learn about the young man, the Royals, the business and so forth."

"I understand that you and Richard were good friends?" asked Holmes.

"That is correct. He and I became very close. His grandmother did not approve of our friendship," said De La Vina. "I cautioned him to be sure and not put his relationship with his grandmother at risk. He didn't listen; he was, like all of the Royals it seems, very hard headed."

"I understand you once worked on the ranch?" asked Holmes.

"Yes, I worked there for many years."

"Did young Richard know of your family's history concerning the ranch?"

"Yes, he did," answered De La Vina. "I did not tell him of it, he learned about it somewhere else."

Holmes looked square into De La Vina's eyes and spoke slowly. "Was he in love with your daughter?"

"Yes, yes he was."

"Where is she now?"

"She is in Spain with family members. She is studying there and has been there for nearly a year."

"So she was not here when Richard disappeared?"

"No."

"Does she know about it?"

"I wrote her a letter. I don't know if she has received it."

"Why did you leave the employ of Mrs. Royal?"

"Mrs. Royal came to see me as a threat to her absolute authority! She thinks she is a queen with absolute power. She found an excuse and she let me go."

"Why did she see you as a threat?" Holmes looked intently at De La Vina. "Had you made any overt threats or actions?"

"Nothing. She knows that even now in Spain there are some who still research old deeds and laws with hope of usurping her claim to the ranch. I am sure she considered me as one of their number."

"I see." Holmes stood and walked towards the fireplace and stood with his back to us. "Do you know anything about what happened to the young man?"

"Nothing. I know nothing."

"Then we shall bid you good night. Thank you for your hospitality." And with that Holmes motioned to us and we made our exit and rode back towards the ranch. It was late and very cool. The clear sky was filled with stars.

As we rode along on our cow ponies Holmes broke the reverie.

"What did you think Watson?"

"I don't think he was telling the truth. Or, at least, not the *whole* truth," I replied.

"I quite agree," said Holmes. "I think he was holding back, there is more he could tell us. I feel we will seeing Don Diego again."

Chapter 22 *Reflections on the case*

We returned to our room and enjoyed a brandy and a cigar, a most excellent Cuban variety, and reflected on the night's work and all of the other pieces of the puzzle.

"So what's next?" I was as puzzled as ever.

"Do you recall seeing a series of gouges in the earth along the creek bed? Those could have been signs of a boat landing and disembarking at some time," said Holmes as he sent up a perfectly round smoke ring.

"That's certainly a possibility but there is no way to know when those were made.

"Quite right. Quite right," said Holmes. "Still, it does fit into one working theory…" His voice tailed off as he become lost in reflection." Did you notice the boat in De La Vina's backyard?

"Why, no."

"No?" Holmes glanced at me with arched eyebrows and an expression that indicated his surprise at my utter incompetence at observation!

"There was a small skiff, about ten or twelve feet in length lying upside down behind his house, a pair of oars was there as well."

"That is interesting."

"Yes, isn't it."

"So have you a theory or a working hypothesis?" I confess I was as much in the dark as ever and could not correlate the known facts into any kind of sense at all.

"Let us outline the facts as we have them." Holmes stood and walked towards the window, his hands clasped behind his back and a most pensive expression fell over his face.

"We know the young man has disappeared. We know it was no accident. We know others are involved, he could not have simply vanished and we know a body was dressed in his clothing and placed on a remote beach, obviously with the intention of deceiving any investigation and throwing it off track. Those are the facts."

"It seems rather a thin line of evidence Holmes."

"Yes but now we may enter into a world of conjecture based on possibilities." Holmes lit up a cigarette and continued his discourse.

"Perhaps someone, with a small boat, met young Royal and conveyed him out into the large bay. From there he could have gone anywhere! We don't know if he aided his own disappearance or whether he was compelled by others."

"So he either was kidnapped or he is involved in some sort of ruse."

"Exactly," said Holmes.

Chapter 23 *Out Into The Laguna Madre*

Following breakfast the next morning Holmes and I, along with Peralta, mounted our horses and were once again off down a trail through some rough brush country. It was a gloriously clear morning with a strong, nippy wind blowing from the north east.

"We need to make good time," said Peralta. "I think maybe this wind from the north may signal a big change in the weather."

With that we picked up our pace a bit as we continued down the trail.

"Ah, this is the life aye Holmes!" I was feeling very much animated by our Wild West experience!

"It is exhilaratingly fascinating," said Holmes. "However I am finding that I miss the teeming intrigue and mass of humanity we have in London!"

"Holmes! It sounds as if you are homesick!"

"Perhaps, just a little," Holmes admitted. "But we are presently engaged and we need to come to a conclusion!"

Up ahead we saw a large body of shallow water and marshlands. The area was covered with small dunes and salt grass was the only vegetation. Various sea birds, gulls, terns and others flittered around and large wading birds, great blue herons, snowy egrets and roseate spoonbills were seen searching for fish in the shallows. Black skimmers were also there as they flew closely above the water with their extended lower beak scooping up tiny crustaceans and other creatures. It was a scene from prehistory and we took it all in.

"Welcome to the *Laguna Madre*," said Peralta.

We rolled out some blankets and sat down to have our lunch, egg and potato *taquitos* with some spicy hot sauce. I was becoming accustomed to and very appreciative of the local fare.

As we ate a pair of coyotes warily came into view but they kept their distance. Holmes suddenly noticed a fairly sizable vessel out in the water,'

"What is that?"

"That is a *Laguna Madre* scow," said Peralta. "Fisherman all along the coast sail these as they cast nets and run traps and lines to catch crabs, fish and shrimp."

As the boat drew nearer we got a better look. The craft was around 30-35 feet in length, very beamy, possibly 10 feet or more and drew very little water which enabled it to sail into areas no regular boat could go. The craft had a low, wide cabin situated near the bow and the large deck behind the cabin was built over a hold for the catch. It had a single mast, stepped just forward of the cabin, with a gaff rigged sail and a jib. It appeared to be a very practical vessel for these waters. As the boat moved by, very close to shore, we waved to the crew onboard. They smiled and waved back. Then Holmes hailed them and motioned for them to pull over to the beach. They did so very smartly and soon an elderly man, skin burned bronze by years of sun and salt, and his young companion scrambled ashore to meet us.

"¡*Hola! Me llamo Capitan Jorge Rivas. El muchacho es mi hijo Juan*," said the boat captain.

After brief salutations and introductions Holmes asked the captain, with Peralta translating, if he might give us a ride out into the bay. An exchange of a few dollars quickly made his mind in the affirmative.

So we boarded the strange craft and shoved off from the bank. The captain sheeted in his sail and we slowly pulled away out into the Laguna Madre. The first thing one quickly discovered about this unusual craft was the smell! Years of dead and dying sea food had imprinted the *La Conchita* with a permanent stench!

The boat was not a swift but it had incredible stability and handled the slight chop which had been building with the increasing wind with no difficulty. Captain Rivas was a skilled handler of his craft and, at Holmes' request, he demonstrated the boat's abilities, sailing on all points of sail, sailing in shallow water and all the while providing a stable platform for the work required onboard.

The temperature was beginning to drop dramatically and Peralta reminded us that we should head to shore in order to return to the ranch house by dark. The captain put us ashore and we mounted up for the return ride. It had been another fascinating experience.

Holmes seemed in rare spirits. As the ranch house came into sight Holmes gave me a mischievous look.

"Watson! Come on, I'll race you to the ranch house!"

With that he flicked the flank of his horse with his quirt and gave a light touch with the spurs and away he flew like a rocket, galloping wildly! Well, of course I quickly gave chase and soon I was galloping after him but he got there first!

Chapter 24 *Return of Mrs. Royal*

After a change of clothes and some hygienic ablutions we had our supper. Mr. Connor Lovejoy, the ranch foreman, was there and he informed us that Mrs. Royal would be returning in the morning and she wanted an early meeting so as to be informed about our progress.

We retired shortly after supper and a brandy and we slept very soundly that night.

The next morning we were summoned to the drawing room after our breakfast and here we encountered Mrs. Royal.

"Mr. Holmes, Dr. Watson, I trust you have been busy in my absence and I would like a report on your progress thus far." Mrs. Royal presented a stern countenance and gave me the distinct impression she was dissatisfied with us. "I have gone to considerable expense to bring you here and you have had a free rein and I want to know now what I have for my expenditures. Have you now a theory or a working plan to find my grandson?"

"Mrs. Royal, I appreciate your anxiety and I can assure you we have been most diligently pursuing the matter and I have two working theories I think as likely possibilities but I still need more facts. There are some aspects of this case that do not easily reveal themselves." Holmes spoke in the calmest and reassuring tone he could muster and it did put Mrs. Royal more at ease.

"Well, I believe you know what you are doing, otherwise I would never have summoned you here."

With that she left us abruptly.

"Watson, I want you to travel to Corpus Christi and check in to the hotel where we stayed. I will meet you there as soon as I can, hopefully by tomorrow evening or the next."

"I will do so," I replied. "Are you on the trail of something?"

"Perhaps," Holmes mused. "I want to satisfy myself on a couple of points that so far seem to be obscured.

After arising early the following morning I made the long, dusty journey back to Corpus Christi. The day was cool and windy but the skies were clear. I checked back into the Hotel Saint Louis and made myself comfortable as I awaited Holmes' arrival.

There was no sign of Holmes that evening or the following two nights. In the morning of the third day I made my way to the hotel dining room for a spot of breakfast. I was heartily enjoying my novel breakfast of *huevos rancheros* and corn *tortillas* when Holmes appeared coming through the door of the restaurant.

"Ah Watson! Breakfast! Hmmm…looks good. I think I will have some." Holmes was in an unusually ebullient mood, especially for in the morning!

"I have been wondering about how you were getting along. So you must have made some good progress," I mused.

The waitress came and Holmes ordered his meal. "I'll have what he is having," said Holmes. We both ordered coffee.

"I have been busy these last days. You would not believe who I saw yesterday! Recall the rather ill-tempered Teutonic gentleman whom we encountered on our crossing?"

"Why yes, a *Herr* Mueller I believe."

"Correct. I saw him as he left the Western Union telegraph office. We did not speak or make eye contact, I don't think he saw me at all." Holmes lit a cigarette and sipped his coffee. "I noticed among the baggage claim checks attached to his luggage, which he had placed on the porch outside the telegraph office, a tag with Mexico D. F. That indicates he did go to Mexico City, which he had stated as his destination when we met aboard ship. The question is, why was he here?"

He continued. "My curiosity was piqued so I sent a telegram to the Pinkerton Agency office in New York City addressed to my old friend Leverton."

"Oh yes, I recall that name," I replied.

"Well, later that evening I returned to the office and found this." Holmes handed me a telegram. "Read it aloud if you will."

"Holmes –stop- I have a dossier on Mr. Mueller-stop-I have here attached it-stop-I hope you come through New York while in US-stop-All the best."

The dossier said Gustav Mueller was in the brewing business and his company was seeking to expand its interests in Mexico. He was named as an agent of the Kaiser Wilhelm's government and had served in the Hesse cavalry during the Franco-Prussian war.

However there was a darker side to Mr. Mueller. Leverton indicated that Mueller often used his brewery business as a cover permitting him to travel and do his work incognito as an *agent provocateur*, that is, as a spy. His whereabouts had been unknown until this message came from Holmes.

"It is indeed odd Watson," said Holmes. It seems the great western powers deem it ungentlemanly to engage in spying so the United States engages a civilian based professional investigative organization, the Pinkertons, to do their dirty work for them and to give them deniability when it suits their purposes. It is a strange world in these times Watson."

Chapter 25 *More Revelations*

"So do you think this Mueller is in some way connected with the Royals or young Richard's disappearance?"

"It doesn't seem likely...and yet...it is a strange coincidence to see him here. And Watson, you know what I think about coincidences."

"Well you must have come up with more than this?"

"Yes, yes I did," Holmes replied. "I am sure you recall the body we viewed that had been dressed in Royal's clothing?"

"Of Course."

"Well. I may possibly have found out who that unfortunate might have been."

Holmes related his actions of the past days. It was, as usual, an incredible tale.

"I donned the guise of a British seaman. The clothes were readily available in a store that featured second hand clothing. I wandered down along the docks where the local fishing fleet tied up and sought some temporary work. I spent two days scraping hulls and mending nets and meeting and talking with the local fishermen. I told them I was looking for a young man I had met on a previous voyage here. Of course I could only give the most vague description but one man I shared lunch time with said he recalled such a man who had only recently arrived here. He said he had sadly drowned in an accident and that his body had not been found. Again, maybe a coincidence but it is possible his body could have been placed on San Jose Island, dressed in young Royal's clothing in order to throw us off the track. I had wondered if murder might have been involved but I think it likely this poor soul was very likely the corpse."

"It reminds me of the case of the Norwood builder in this respect," I interjected.

"Yes, there are certain similarities although murder was involved in that sad story." Holmes said. He continued.

"A narrative has been building in my mind Watson and, though all of the evidence is mostly very circumstantial, it is hanging together nicely. However there remain questions I don't yet have answers for. I fear Mrs. Royal may run out of patience soon so I feel I must redouble my efforts."

"So what do you think?" I asked.

"I think young Royal staged his disappearance, with the help of confederates, and he is still in this area, hiding out, waiting for an opportunity to travel to Spain to marry his sweetheart."

Chapter 26 *It's The Same All Over*

"This breakfast is uncommonly good this morning Watson!" said Holmes as he attacked the eggs, sausage and *tortillas* complete with an ample serving of hot *salsa.*

I demonstrated my agreement as I too wolfed down our South Western repast.

"I am beginning to like this style of food Watson."

Holmes surprised me with that remark.

"It is odd, is it not, that here we sit, nearly three thousand miles from home, in an environment totally alien to us and yet we see the same traits of petty jealousness, dishonesty, criminality and all of the other characteristics that the human race is yet to leave behind as evolution progresses."

"Yes it is Holmes. I observed much the same when I was stationed in India and Afghanistan. Humans do seem to be basically the same around the world."

We were interrupted by the appearance of a boy shouting "Telegram for Mr. Sherlock Holmes! Telegram for Mr. Sherlock Holmes."

"Here boy!" Holmes stood and took the telegram as he slipped the boy a few coins. "Thank you."

"My telegram! It came much sooner than I anticipated. This is from Leverton. He told me he would be sending more on Mr. Mueller."

Holmes looked at the telegram and, though he attempted to conceal it, an expression of astonishment spread over his countenance. He thrust it at me.

"Read this!"

"Holmes, if at all possible keep an eye on Muller and note his activities and contacts – stop – Two agents have been dispatched post haste – stop- Should arrive within the week – stop – You will be paid for your efforts – stop - Will be in touch – stop – Leverton

"What do you suppose?" I pondered this strange missive.

"I don't know Watson. It is intriguing!"

Holmes gestured toward the crumpled copy of the *San Antonio Light* newspaper on the table. "So have you been able to keep up with events at home the last few days while you waited for me?"

"Well, this paper has a few columns on Europe but not much. I did see where the Hague Conventions were not agreed to and the talks fell apart," I replied.

"That doesn't bode well, and as we both know. all of Europe is an armed camp and dangerous and entangling alliances have been made which could but a spark to explode at any time." said Holmes. "What else of interest did you find?"

"It seems that Mexico has been long under the tyrannical rule of Porfirio Diaz and much of Mexico, especially in the north, is close to armed rebellion."

"Anything else?"

"Yes," I replied. The American Department of State, the equivalent of our Foreign Office, has issued a series of protests to the German government accusing them of violating the Monroe Doctrine by sticking their nose in Mexican affairs in an attempt to gain influence and to extend their presence into this hemisphere."

"It seems the old world is loath to change its ways in the new one!" Holmes exclaimed.

Chapter 27 *The Plot Thickens*

"Well Watson, I think you should return to the ranch and placate Mrs. Royal. She seems to be growing short of patience with us," Said Holmes with a look meant to instill confidence.

"But what will I tell her?" I implored.

"Well, tell her we are making rapid progress and we should soon bring this lamentable affair to an end."

"Oh?" I said. "Is that true?"

"Yes, I think it is true. I feel we are very warm at the moment and soon all will be revealed."

"If you say so." I wasn't so confident as Holmes appeared to be.

With that exchange we concluded breakfast and Holmes departed after telling me he would be back at the ranch in no more than two days.

I was able to get a ticket for the afternoon train that evening I found I was in time for dinner. Mrs. Royal joined me and, after some rather chilly conversation, she asked about Holmes' whereabouts.

"Forgive me Dr. Watson but I must have some news of yours and Mr. Holmes' activities. I have gone to enormous trouble and expense and this has just been seemingly dragging along!" Mrs. Royal was plainly perturbed.

"Mrs. Royal, please calm yourself. Don't get over wrought. I have seen Holmes work seeming miracles. He is capable of making sense when all others see nothing but confusion and haze," I spoke in my best bedside manner. "Holmes assures me we will soon see a resolution."

"Thank you Doctor. I think I will retire now. Good evening to you sir," she said morosely as she walked up the stairs.

"Well, that went well!" I said to myself.

The weather was turning cooler again and I sat by the fire for a while, enjoyed a brandy and did some reading on Mexican history.

The following morning after breakfast I thought I would go out for a ride. Soon Peralta appeared with my mount and the two of us set off on the trail which led to the river. It was a bracing morning with a stiff north wind raking us but the sky was clear.

"Peralta, do you still have family living in Mexico?"

"Oh *sí señor*," he replied.

"Do you see them often?"

"Not often, but sometimes I go there and sometimes some of them have been here for a visit," he answered.

"So what do you think of the President, Mr. Diaz?"

Peralta fell silent for a while. Then he spoke, slowly "He is a very bad man. He is a, how you say? A *dictador*!" He grimaced and spat on the ground for emphasis. He continued, "There is big trouble coming soon in *Mexico*. Soon there will be *revolución*. It will be very bloody I fear."

"That sounds serious. So there opposition to Diaz?"

"A man, Francisco Madero, is leading an opposition movement and he is gathering much support. The next election will be *muy importante*" For many years the elections have been rigged; maybe this one will be different. But Diaz has already said he would not heed the results if he was not re-elected. If that happens it will be *revolución*."

"I hope nothing of the kind occurs," I replied though I feared that he knew what he was talking about. "Mexico is a very poor country is it not> It could not well afford such violence."

No *señor*, it could not but Mexico has a long and violent history from *La Conquista* when Hernan Cortes and his Spanish *conquistadores* conquered *Las Aztecas* to the *revolución* against the Spanish inspired by Father Hidalgo and his *Grito del Delores, Mexicanos* still resent very much the invasion by *Los Estados Unidos* when Mexico lost two thirds of her territory. You know that where we are now was considered to be Mexico only 62 years ago. Porfirio Diaz himself said *"Pobre Mexico! Tan cerca de los Estados Unidos, tan lejos del Dios!* So close to the United States, so far from God!"

I understood a smattering of Spanish but I was improving while here. From those remarks I understood the meaning, "Poor Mexico! So far from God, so close to the United States!"

Peralta continued "Then there was the invasion of the French also, when Napoleon III installed Maximilian of Austria-Hungry as emperor of Mexico. This sparked the revolution led by Benito

Juarez and Diaz was one of his main generals. He was a national hero then."

"Let us pray matters will be resolved peacefully and democratically," I said.

"Something else you should know doctor. There is strong feeling, especially in the army, of which Diaz is also the head, that someday Mexico should reclaim its lost territory from the United States."

None of this portends well for the near future I thought to myself

Chapter 28 *Message From Mueller*

The next morning I received a message from Holmes. "Watson, go by De La Vina's cabin and see if he is there. If he is talk with him a while ask a few questions, I am sure you will think of something. If he is not there then come back to Corpus Christi and check back into the hotel. I will see you soon. Holmes."

In short order I was at De La Vina's place, accompanied once again by Peralta. De la Vina was not there. I promptly returned to our room, packed a bag, took train passage once again to Corpus Christi and checked back into the Hotel Saint Louis. The desk clerk had a message for me.

"Watson," It read. "I will join you in the hotel restaurant for dinner. In the meantime take the short walk down Water Street and proceed to Jones' Livery and Blacksmith Shop. Look for a roan gelding with white stockinged feet and a silver blaze on the forehead. If you see such a horse, in a very discreet manner, inquire as to whom brought that horse to the shop and when.

Will see you soon.

Holmes"

I did as Holmes said and went to the livery. There I found a large, garrulous man by the name of Jones busily in the process of shoeing a horse.

He saw me enter and asked if he could be of service.

"Wait a moment and I'll be right with ya," he said.

So I sat on a crude wooden bench and watched as he deftly finished nailing a shoe on a horse's foot. When he finished he approached, wiping his hands on a grimy leather apron.

"Now what can I do for you sir."

"Well, I saw a nice looking roan gelding the other day and I was interested in purchasing it. I see you have it here in your enclosure."

"You aint from around here are ya?"

"No, no I am not. I am from England and I am visiting your fascinating state."

"Oh. Well thet horse aint mine. He is just being kept here for a while. I often board folk's horses while they are in town."

"I see. Could you tell me who owns the horse and where I might find him?"

"Well I don't rightly know. He paid cash up front and I don't ask too many questions. Tell you what though, I 'spect he'll be back here real soon. He said he would pick up the horse at sunset."

"Thanks, Perhaps I will return."

"I wouldn't be real concerned mister. I can make you a real good deal on a much better horse than that one."

"Well, thank you. I'll see."

With that exchange I took my leave. I came back about a quarter hour before sunset. It was starting to get cold but fortunately I didn't have to wait long before I saw De La Vina leading the horse from the stable. So it was his horse. He mounted and I followed him for a while at a discreet distance until I saw him take the road leading west, out of town. Feeling very satisfied with my surveillance work I returned to the hotel.

As good as his word, Holmes appeared at my table in the hotel restaurant just as I was preparing to order dinner.

"Well, Watson! Did you find out anything today?" Holmes was in an ebullient mood.

"Why yes, Holmes," I said. "I discovered something interesting. De La Vina had his horse kept at the livery you sent me to. I saw him pick it up and ride off."

"Excellent Watson!" This was great praise from Holmes!

"I too had a good day. I observed your hopelessly inadequate surveillance of Mueller. You don't know where he went? You don't know what he was doing do you?" Holmes cast a sideways glance my way as he made his impertinent remark!

"Really Holmes! Such a remark is entirely uncalled for!" I was stung by Holmes' attitude but I resolved to show a good face! You say you observed me?"

"Yes, do you recall seeing a *peón* sitting in the shade nearby with his *burro*?"

"That was *you* Holmes?" Once again Holmes had astonished me, something he loved to do! "So what did you find out that I missed?"

"Read this," He handed me a telegram.

"It's in German Holmes! I am afraid my German isn't up to it," I protested.

"Oh yes, quite. I'll read it. My German is quite good."

Holmes read it, translating as he went along. It read:

Hans,

I have found someone who is willing to help. He wants help from us. He has lost his cow and wants us to help him get it back.

Pieter

"What do you make of that Watson?"

"Why it sounds like childish gibberish!"

"Yes, yes it does. But be assured there is meaning there. It is obviously a cypher, though a mediocre one at best, the sender must have had little expectation that anyone would be reading his correspondence" said Holmes with a pensive expression clouding his face.

Holmes lit a cigar, he had developed a fondness for Cubans. As he blew a large swirl of smoke which slowly swirled towards the ceiling two well-dressed gentlemen approached.

"Mr. Holmes I presume?" One of them extended his hand which we both took and shook, he had a firm grip I noticed.

"I am Morris Judson and this is my colleague Bob Livingston. We are from the Pinkerton Agency. Leverton sent us."

"Ah Leverton!" Holmes indicated they should sit down. "Gentlemen, please."

Chapter 29 *The Trail Grows Warm*

Livingston was carrying a leather attaché which was fastened with a light chain locked to his wrist! Quite novel I thought. He took a small key and unlocked the attaché and placed it on the table. From within he produced several files stuffed with documents.

"Here are our files on Muller and Mr. De La Vina and others here in South Texas. You will find here information on a number of German nationals as well as Americans of German origin, some are immigrants and many are born citizens. There is a character here by the name of Prince Soms, who claims to be Austrian nobility though we have our doubts. He has for some time been agitating for an independence movement of sorts whereby those of German extraction might form their own nation here in Texas or possibly as an autonomous state of Mexico.

Fortunately the vast majority of the German-American population wants nothing to do with the Kaiser and is very happy to be loyal to their adopted country."

"Fascinating!" Holmes was very animated. I could see his interest was piqued.

"Furthermore," said Judson, "We have direct communications from Mueller to the Kaiser Wilhelm himself. It is amazing he did not think it necessary to conceal his meaning but here they are."

Holmes looked these documents over rapidly but I knew he was digesting the information in his efficient brain. He handed them over to me.

Then Holmes selected on formal looking document and held in front of his face.

"This communique, gentlemen, is the heart of the matter is it not? Watson read this aloud."

He handed it to me, It had an English translation on a separate page, as they all did.

"Good God! This is preposterous!" What I read here was shocking beyond imagination.

"Why this could mean war! It is a promise to Mexico that if that country should align itself with Imperial Germany and support Germany in any future conflict, which they intimate could occur at any time, that in the eventuality of victory by Germany, and her allies in the Central Powers, that to Mexico all territories lost to the United States in the preceding century would henceforth be returned to Mexico and that Mexico would then grant to Germany trade, mineral and natural resource concessions. In such eventuality Germany would provide troops, weapons and naval forces for the protection of Mexico against all enemies, including the United States."

"Quite a bold proposal." Said Holmes. "This could inalterably affect the balance of power and do immeasurable harm to chances for peace in Europe or indeed in the entire world!"

"So you see clearly why our government views this matter with such concern," said Judson.

"Indeed!" Holmes was obviously affected.

"So what does De La Vina have to do with all of this?" I was puzzled.

"Well, you know De La Vina was resentful that his family interest in the Royal Ranch had been usurped, in his eyes anyway. He saw a chance here to have his family's Royal Spanish land grant to be reinstated. That would be sufficient motivation I think," said Holmes.

"So what now?" I asked.

"I have an idea," said Holmes.

Holmes wrote down two messages and handed them to Judson. "Send these right away," he said.

Judson looked them over. One was to Mueller, it read "Come to my cabin tomorrow evening. Don't be seen."

The other to De La Vina, "I am coming to your place tomorrow night. Make sure you are alone. I want to see the boy."

So you think De La Vina can produce the young man?"

"I am sure of it," said Holmes.

Chapter 30 *Confrontation*

"Here is my plan," said Holmes. "We will leave early tomorrow morning, before sunrise. It will be cool so we must be prepared. We will proceed to the vicinity of De La Vina's cabin and conceal ourselves well before dusk. When Mueller arrives I will stealthily position myself near the side window, to the left of the cabin, so I might be able to hear their conversation. When I give the signal the rest of you will rush the door, with pistols drawn. We must not give either man an opportunity to resist. Any suggestions? Any other thoughts?"

"We will follow your lead Mr. Holmes. Your plan is a sound one I think," said Judson.

"I agree," added Livingston.

Sleep that night proved elusive, as it often did as a climactic moment loomed, one that might conclude or throw into pieces the fruits of a stressful and lengthy investigation. Eventually, however, I did fall off to a sound slumber.

I was awakened in the pre-dawn hours by a gentle shaking and the old familiar phrase which never failed to electrify me. "Watson, the game is afoot!"

I trundled out of bed and soon we were down in the hotel restaurant, joined by Judson and Livingston, enjoying a hearty breakfast of *huevos rancheros, migas* and corn *tortillas*, washed down by strong coffee.

Holmes encouraged us. "Eat heartily men, it may be some time before our next hot meal!"

We took with us a bag full of *taquitos* and *tortilla* chips along with a large jar of *salsa*.

Soon we were out of town and we rode along in silence, raked by a chilling north wind which felt as if it cut right through to the bone. It was more uncomfortable than I had expected. I pulled my jacket tightly closed and endured until, at long last, we drew near De La Vina's place. Here we took off the trail and found a small clearing in the brush where we lit a small fire and made a pot of coffee and ate some of our "grub" as our companions called it. We dug a pit for the fire and extinguished it as soon as we had some good coals to use. We were apprehensive that De La Vina or Mueller might see the fire smoke but the nourishment was bracing. Soon it was dark and we positioned ourselves closer to the cabin. We had left our horses in an *arroyo*, a kind of gulley, where they were hobbled and left with feed. The sun had gone down now and Holmes whispered "No talking now. At my signal we will execute our plan."

We nodded in agreement and took out places. The night fell quickly but in the dark time slowed, only the punctuation of lonesome coyote calls and unseen wings broke the silence.

I fought off slumber until I was electrified by a sudden intrusion of another sound. A Horse! I could hear the slow approach of a horse. Immediately I was alert. I placed my hand on my revolver and watched. Then a horse and rider appeared out of the gloom. The rider dismounted and tied the reins to a hitching post in front of the cabin. He knocked on the door. And it opened, revealing De la Vina with a lamp in his hand. The man entered and almost immediately Holmes appeared at the door with his ear pressed against it. Holmes turned his head in my direction and pressed his index finger to his lips. He motioned me to be still with his other hand. For a moment all was suspended as I awaited the next move. It came with suddenness as Holmes forced open the door and trundled into the room. I followed instantly and a few seconds later our American colleagues followed. All had pistols drawn. You might imagine the effect this had on the inhabitants of the cabin as De La Vina and Mueller stared at us with wide eyes and shock on their faces.

Mueller was the first to react. He leaped to his feet. "What is the meaning of this…this outrage!"

Holmes looked at the men with a stony expression. "There is no reason to be alarmed. You will not be injured in the least…if you co-operate."

Muller sat back down.

"Señor Holmes! Doctor Watson! Why are you doing this? What do you want?" De La Vina was genuinely shocked.

As our eyes became accustomed to the dim light within the cabin we became aware of a third figure. It was a man whose terrified eyes stared out from his grimy face. He was very thin, disheveled and filthy. His hands were bound tightly behind his back and a gag was wrapped around his head passing through his mouth.

"This must be Richard Royal III," said Holmes. He approached the man and quickly freed him of his bonds.

"Oh help me! Help me! These men want to kill me!" He became very emotional.

Holmes placed his left arm around the man's shoulder. "Do not fret. Your ordeal is over. You will be brought to safety and we will see these men are brought to justice."

We were joined by Judson and Livingston. They produced handcuffs and clamped them onto the two miscreants.

'I remember you!" snarled Muller. "You and your friend there are those arrogant Englishman I encountered on the Atlantic voyage. By what authority do you detain us?"

"Allow me to present myself once again. I am Sherlock Holmes, consulting detective, London and this is my esteemed colleague Dr. Watson, also of London and our American counterparts, Mr. Morris Judson and Mr. Bob Livingston, Pinkerton agents."

I clicked my heels and made a slight bow in what I hoped was a mockery of the Prussian style.

"Again! By what authority do you detain us? You are not proper representatives of the law here!"

"Contain yourself Mueller," Holmes' voice dripped contempt. "You are wrong sir. We are working with the governments of the United States, Great Britain and the state of Texas,"

"Sir, we have a multitude of charges, including murder and kidnapping and I have listed them here if you care to see it," said Livingston.

"And you De La Vina!" Holmes pointed an accusatory finger. "Betraying a young man you had befriended since his childhood.

Even involving your own daughter in this despicable scheme of yours."

"I don't know what you are talking about!" De La Vina spoke loudly but unconvincingly.

"You lure young Royal with the promise of a secret meeting with your daughter. You knew he would come immediately. You knew he would say nothing to anyone, as you had instructed. He helped you drag your boat to the creek where he hid himself under a net as you proceeded out into the bay where he was placed on board one of the fishing scows which took him to Aransas Pass. All the while he trusted you and never imagined you were to betray him," Holmes was biting in his accusations. He continued as De La Vina appeared more downcast.

"Royal was then placed in irons and kept in an old cellar by your confederates there. Mueller was brought into the scheme as he was seeking support among local Mexicans for the return of these lands to Mexico and an alliance with Germany. When you informed Muller about the kidnapping, rather than being shocked Muller saw this as a card, an ace in the hole so to speak, to be played later. However Muller demonstrated on our previous meeting that he was a poor poker player."

"I wish to contact my embassy. I am protected by diplomatic immunity! I protest!" Mueller was livid. "Preposterous!"

"Come on! All in good time. Now move!" Livingston gave both of them a sharp push in the back to get them moving out the door. "Now sit on the ground and keep quiet!"

I examined Royal and found him to be in a shocking condition. He was emaciated, dirty and carrying a touch of fever. He seemed to be in a mild state of shock but I felt he would soon recover with proper rest and nourishment.

"Watson, go to the Royal Ranch and report what has happened and return with a buckboard and a horse for young Royal here. We will await your return." Holmes, as always, was cool and collected.

Chapter 31 *End Of The Trail*

I rushed back to the ranch house as fast as I could get my horse to go and there roused the occupants. I also contacted the local sheriff's office and they said they would send deputies to make an official arrest. As one might imagine Mrs. Royal was immediately enervated and she drove her men to collect the necessary equipage and soon we flying pell mell back to the cabin.

The first streaks of dawn were now visible in the high clouds on this cold morning. As we arrived. Mrs. Royal fairly flew to her grandson's side.

"Oh Richard! I feared we would never see you again!" She tearfully embraced her grandson. "Bring the buckboard up! Load him into it. Careful. Here are some blankets, just lay still Richard. Soon we will be home and we will get you some coffee and some food."

Quickly our entire assemblage now rapidly headed back to the ranch. I was getting rather used to galloping along these rugged trails!

On our arrival the cook quickly brewed up several pots of strong, black coffee and whipped up an amazing quantity of eggs, bacon and biscuits! It seemed miraculous. The victuals, or "vittles," as they called the food was very welcome after a long, tension filled night on the cold wind.

I observed some new visitors riding up. About six men, all heavily armed, had just tied their horse to the hitching posts.

These were lawmen, come to take Mueller and De La Vina into custody.

Deputy Tom Mitchell, of the Royal County Sheriff's Department stepped forward and instructed his men to get the prisoners mounted and secured.

"So you found your grandson! Well now that's a right good thing Mrs. Royal. I am glad for you," said Mitchell.

"No thanks to you Mitchell," Mrs. Royal fairly snarled.

Mitchell was unfazed by her outburst, obviously they were well acquainted. "Hell I know this one! It's old De La Vina. Don't know this other rascal. Don't worry we will keep them safely in our jail until they go to trial,"

Following breakfast we were ushered into the dining room Mrs. Royal produced her finest brandy,

"Gentlemen! A toast! To The safe return of Richard." She held high her glass and we all joined her. "And now Mr. Holmes, Doctor Watson, please join me in my study and we will settle up." Mrs. Royal was not one to let grass grow under her feet!

She sat at her large, engraved and handmade oaken desk and opened the top drawer. She produced a small, flat banking bag. "Here is expense money for your return trip."

She then withdrew a black leather checkbook, embossed with her initials in gold. She quickly wrote out a check and handed it to Holmes. "I hope this is sufficient for your services." Holmes looked at the check. His eyebrows rose, almost imperceptibly and his eyes widened just so slightly. I was very familiar with Holmes' mannerisms and I knew he was impressed.

"This is a king's ransom!" Holmes said.

"You have given me back my future Mr. Holmes."

"Thank you," he said quietly as he slipped the check into his inside jacket pocket.

Chapter 32 *Return Home*

We enjoyed an American holiday before we left. Thanksgiving was celebrated recognizing a group of religious refugees which had fled England in the early 17th century, they called them the pilgrims, a sect of dissenters who were similar to the Puritans but they were separatists, that is, they wanted a break from the Church of England. They were bound for Virginia but by miscalculation they landed in Massachusetts in 1620. The following year, after much hardship, they celebrated their success in forming their colony with a large feast of all the bounty of their harvest and with fresh meat provided by the local Indians who joined in their feast and a day of thanksgiving was declared.

So we joined in on the feast and walked long tables, set with gorgeous table cloths and decorations, and piled high with huge helpings of roast turkey, sweet hams, mashed potatoes, gravy, stuffing, rolls, yams, cranberry sauce, and a delightful fruit salad called ambrosia, indeed the food of the gods! And there was more! Cakes, pies and other sweets and pastries were there. And of course a table held *enchiladas, tamales* and *tortillas* galore. This was all washed down with gallons of iced tea and everyone from ranch hands to the Royals stuffed themselves to the point of discomfort. Following the meal the participants relaxed, told stories and consumed various libations, ranging from fine Mexican brandy to beer, wine and, of course, *tequila.*

A group of the ranch hands and their families had formed a *mariachi* band which thrilled the gathering with a selection of *Musica Ranchera.*

Dressed in resplendent *Charro* costumes, complete with large, elaborately embroidered *sombreros*, The musicians played an assortment of trumpets, guitars, violins and guitar-like instruments, a *bajo sexto* and a *guitarrón.* There was a male and a female lead singer and most of the musicians sang back up choruses. The songs were rousing numbers with titles such as *Ay Jalisco, Cielito Lindo* and *La Cucaracha.* Holmes was well impressed with the violin playing, "I wonder if I might be able to purchase recordings of this type of music?" he mused. I just nodded, unenthusiastically I might add, and shrugged my shoulders. "*¿Quien sabe?*" I was showing off my newly acquired skills in linguistics!

The next morning we said our goodbyes and set out for San Antonio, there to take the Southern-Pacific railroad to Chicago and on to New York where we would once again cross the North Atlantic. We weren't eager for a crossing this time of year but better now than later in the winter. We enjoyed the panoramic view the train ride afforded. This was a remarkable country and so very large! In New York we visited with Leverton ever so briefly and then we were off on our return voyage.

On board ship, as we watched the Statue of Liberty slide away over the horizon, we toasted our Texas adventure.

"I can't wait to see Mrs. Hudson and once again enjoy her wonderful home cooking," I said.

Holmes chuckled. "Watson, all you think about is food! I can't help but wonder what kind of mess Lestrade has gotten himself into. It will be good to be home again!"

Also from Dicky Neely

A century after the publication of The Hound of the Baskervilles, the relevance of both Sherlock Holmes and Dr. John H. Watson is jeopardised. Their creator, Sir Arthur Conan Doyle is accused of stealing the narrative for the supreme adventure from a friend called Bertram Fletcher Robinson. Worse still, it is also alleged that Sir Arthur committed adultery, blackmail and murder in order to conceal his act of plagiarism. The stage is now been for the return of Holmes and Watson to Dartmoor in Devon!

Also from MX Publishing

MX Publishing is proud to support the campaign to save and restore Sir Arthur Conan Doyle's former home. Undershaw is where he brought Sherlock Holmes back to life, and should be preserved for future generations of Holmes fans.

Save Undershaw   www.saveundershaw.com

Facebook   www.facebook.com/saveundershaw

You can read more about Sir Arthur Conan Doyle and Undershaw in Alistair Duncan's book (share of royalties to the Undershaw Preservation Trust) – An Entirely New Country and in the amazing compilation Sherlock's Home – The Empty House (all royalties to the Trust).

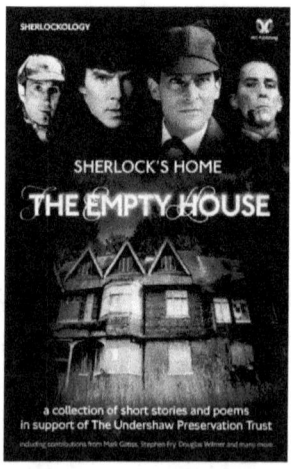

Also from MX Publishing

More short story Sherlock Holmes collections

The Oustanding Mysteries of Sherlock Holmes
(Gerard Kelly)

The Untold Adventure of Sherlock Holmes
(Luke Kuhns)

www.mxpublishing.com

Also from MX Publishing

Cross over fiction featuring great villains from history

Fantasy Sherlock Holmes

www.mxpublishing.com

Also from MX Publishing

Carrying the seal of the Conan Doyle Estate…..

On the most secret and dangerous assignment of their lives, Sherlock Holmes and Dr. Watson are sent into the newborn Soviet Union to rescue The Romanovs: Nicholas and Alexandra and their innocent children. Will Holmes and Watson be able to change history? Will they even be able to survive?

www.ingramcontent.com/pod-product-compliance
Lightning Source LLC
Chambersburg PA
CBHW071325130626
46556CB00004B/1758